The Tale of Little Slytherly Witherly

William J. Smith

AuthorHouse™
1663 Liberty Drive
Bloomington, IN 47403
www.authorhouse.com
Phone: 1-800-839-8640

©2011 William J. Smith. All rights reserved.

No part of this book may be reproduced, stored in a retrieval system,
or transmitted by any means without the written permission of the author.

First published by AuthorHouse 6/16/2011

ISBN: 978-1-4567-5672-7 (sc)

Library of Congress Control Number: 2011907912

Printed in the United States of America

Any people depicted in stock imagery provided by Thinkstock are models,
and such images are being used for illustrative purposes only.
Certain stock imagery © Thinkstock.

This book is printed on acid-free paper.

Because of the dynamic nature of the Internet, any web addresses or links contained
in this book may have changed since publication and may no longer be valid. The views
expressed in this work are solely those of the author and do not necessarily reflect the
views of the publisher, and the publisher hereby disclaims any responsibility for them.

The tale of little **Slytherly Witherly** begins the same as all other stories. He was brought into this world through love between his mother and father. However, his world is much larger than ours, for he is ten times smaller than any child. For he lives among the grass beneath our feet, taking the same journey as us through life.

Once little Slytherly was old enough to walk, his father took him to watch the local game of slingball. Venturing through the blades of grass they came to an opening, where little Slytherly was able to see the game being played.
After grabbing a local meal, A Cup O' Dirt, they marched closer to the arena.
"Son," his father said leaning over towards him, "I used to play this game when I was younger with passion, love, and respect. Maybe one day you can too."
After hearing this, a big smile swept across little Slytherly, filling him with joy.

"What a great game that was, Father," little Slytherly said passionately.   After the game, they walked in the grass exploring areas Slytherly had never seen before.

His father, wanting to share his dreams with little Slytherly, told him of the story of venturing to The Great Tree.

"One day, when all is ready, and you are old enough to make the journey. We will pack up our things and leave this home."

Should his father or shouldn't his father tell little Slytherly the dangers ahead. This is the struggle his father felt. However, his father felt it best to educate him of those dangers.

"Many others have made this journey," his father began, "But few survive." Little Slytherly's smile began to fade.

"The big, glowing ball in the sky can heat the rock-like surface beneath us and the unbearable heat can steal the life from you. So, we must stick to the dirt and grass trails."

"Although, there is another way," His father said with concern, "Down the river towards the Black Hole, but this is far too dangerous for someone as young as you."

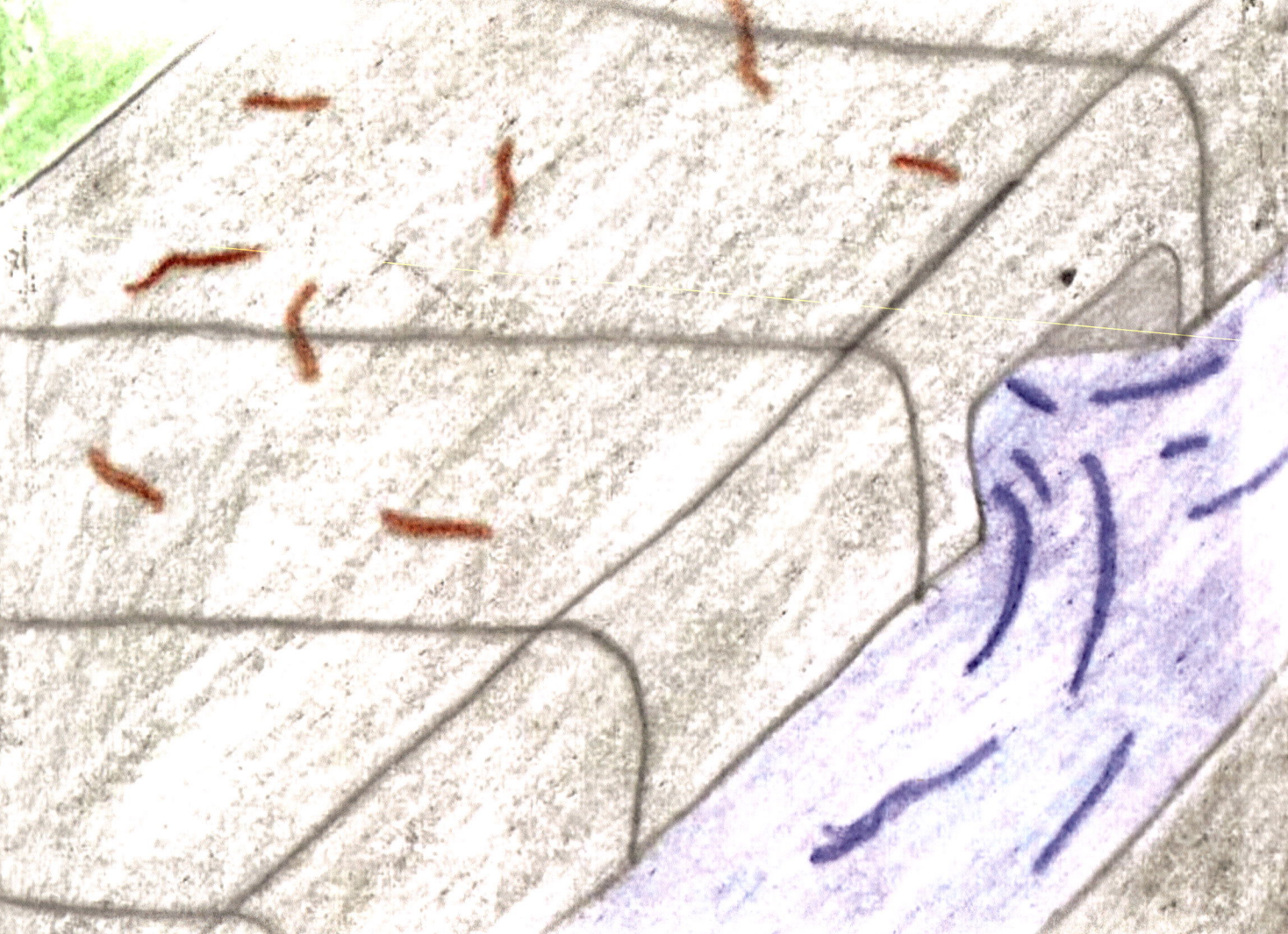

Not wanting to further discuss the horror that came with the Black Hole, he quickly changed the subject.

"Well, I think that is enough stories for now, your mother has a surprise waiting for you."

Smiling once again, they left for home.

Walking through the blades of grass, Little Slytherly daydreamed of the stories his father told him. "What could be so bad about the Black Hole?" he questioned.

Approaching his home, Little Slytherly saw that a group of critters were gathering. When suddenly, they began singing "Happy Birthday" to him.

Looking around to see who came to his birthday, little Slytherly saw Big Uncle Witherly, also Mr. Ant and his family.

Once his birthday party was over, Little Slytherly went to bed that night dreaming happily.

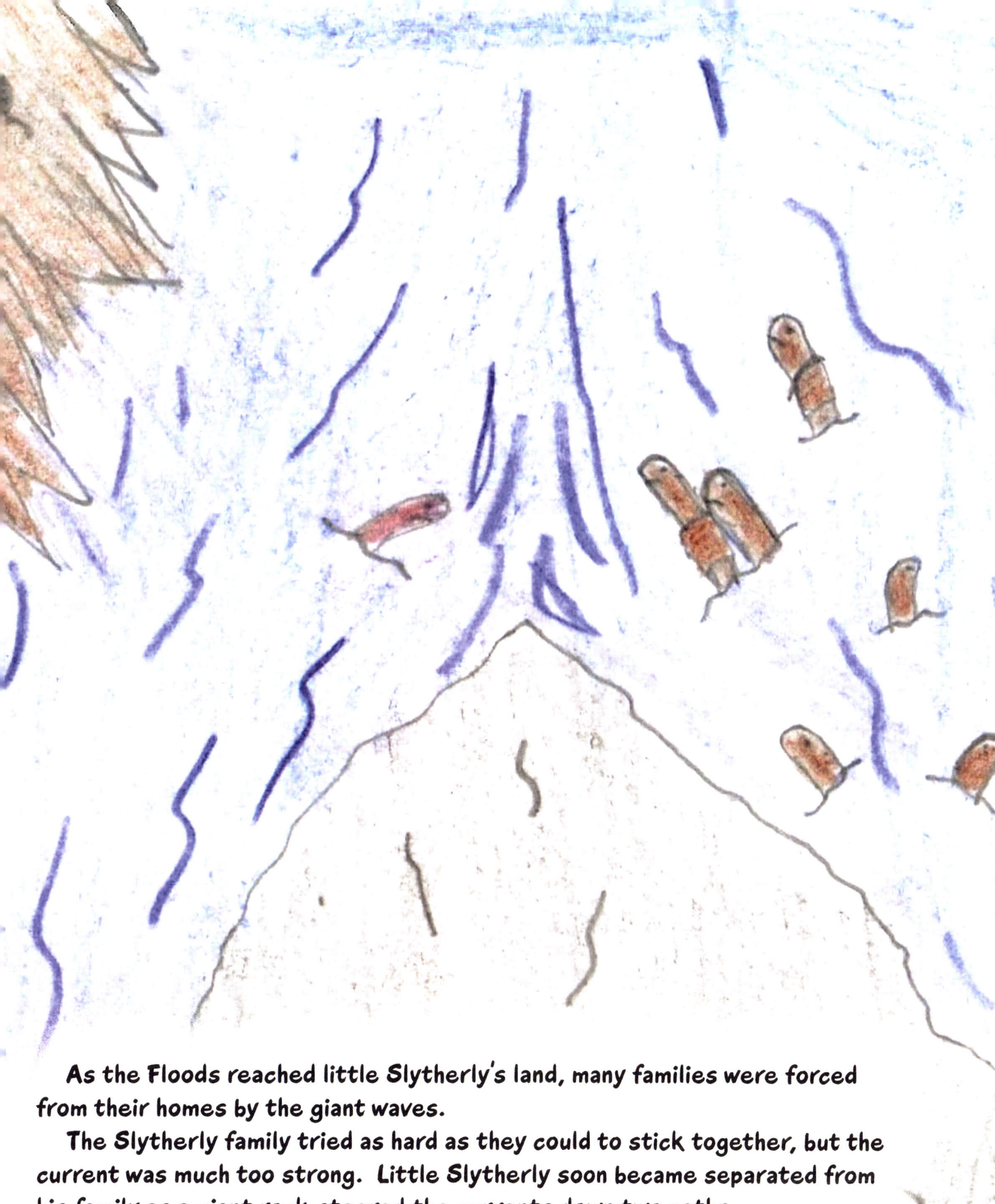

   As the Floods reached little Slytherly's land, many families were forced from their homes by the giant waves.
   The Slytherly family tried as hard as they could to stick together, but the current was much too strong. Little Slytherly soon became separated from his family as a giant rock steered the currents down two paths.

Stranded alone under a leaf, protected from the rain, little Slytherly grew afraid of what the future might bring him. For this is the first time he has been in the wilderness alone.

"What do I do?" Little Slytherly asked himself. "I have no idea where I am or where my parents are."

With nothing but questions running through his mind, he lowered his head to the ground thinking of what he should do.

Lying under his leaf, a thought occurred to him: "Maybe my parents are heading to The Great Tree, hoping I would do the same?"

Little Slytherly's hopes began to rise, and he decided to act on this thought. Perhaps little Slytherly could even beat his parents there.

"How do I get there?" He asked himself while looking around. "I know... I'll ride this leaf down the river until I reach The Great Tree!"

Shoving the leaf off the rock-like surface, he then leaped off for an adventure!

A smiling Little Slytherly drifted down the river with hopes and happiness swarming around him. As waves crashed up against his leaf, his thought of being with his family brought good feelings.

"I wonder what kind of friends I will make? What kind of new games to learn and enjoy? Oh, I sure hope they have slingball!"

Growing restless of waiting for all the fun that awaited him at The Great Tree, he soon forgot how sad he was just moments ago.

Cruising down the watery jet-way, little Slytherly saw something dark in the distance.

"Could this be the Black Hole my father was telling me about?" He questioned.

Thinking with haste, little Slytherly needed to plan a strategy on how to avoid being swallowed by the Black Hole.

"I know! As soon as I reach the edge of the Black Hole, I will jump off of my leaf and land onto the rock-like surface. Then I can make my journey into the grass."

Bracing himself, little Slytherly prepared to leap for safety. Disaster struck!

A massive tidal wave collided with his leaf; he saw his escape plan vanish right before him.

Not knowing what to expect next, little Slytherly began to fear that maybe he might not be able to reunite with his family.

Sweeping into the black hole, all plans of escape lost, little Slytherly had to act quickly.

With all hopes shattered, he saw what he thought to be a solid, rock-like surface inside the black hole, and he jumped.

Clinging to the hard rock-like surface with what little strength he could, he began to pull himself to safety.

Narrowly escaping what disaster might have brought him, little Slytherly grew faint with exhaustion.

Growing more tired by the second, little Slytherly struggled to keep his eyes open. Everything around him became blurry and out of focus. But out of the corner of his eye, he saw a shadow creeping closer to him.

Not knowing what this shadow was, fear swept over him to stay awake. Shifting violently side to side to wake himself up, he made an attempt to stand.

But it was too late for little Slytherly, exhaustion became his enemy. Falling to the ground, he soon fell fast asleep.

Slowly, little Slytherly's eyes began to open. Dazed, his eyes saw a big, blurry, and green object breathing in the corner.

Sliding away, he saw on his other side another creature, bursting with colors. Red . . . blue . . . green . . . and even orange covered this creature.

Fearful for his safety, little Slytherly gathered what strength he could find and backed himself into a corner.

That's when he heard a deep, low voice begin to speak, "Feisty young one, he is."

"It's okay little one," said a sweet innocent voice. "Your safe now, but you almost got swept away by the river."

Finally, little Slytherly's eyes cleared, and he was able to see again. "Who are you?" he questioned.

"Call me Mr. Slug," commanded the deep voice.

"I'm Jasmine," said the sweet voice.

After introducing themselves, and telling how they all came to this place, Jasmine shared her story with little Slytherly. How she was going to become a butterfly one day and live with all the critters at The Great Tree.

Little Slytherly questioned them on how they were going to escape the black hole.

"Once the river dies down, we are going to journey out of here and up the rock-like surface. But we must travel quickly before the rock-like surface heats up, which will be no good." Mr. Slug told them.

As the night grew old, little Slytherly began dreaming again of life at The Great Tree.

However, little did Mr. Slug and little Slytherly know that it was time for Jasmine to cocoon herself in a deep sleep that night.

"It's time," said Mr. Slug, awaking little Slytherly from his sleep.

Upon awakening, little Slytherly saw that Jasmine had cocooned herself while they slept last night.

"What should we do?" He asked Mr. Slug.

"It was her time, but we must carry on before it becomes too hot outside." Mr. Slug said sternly.

Dragging Jasmine by her cocoon, little Slytherly hoped that he was not causing her any harm.

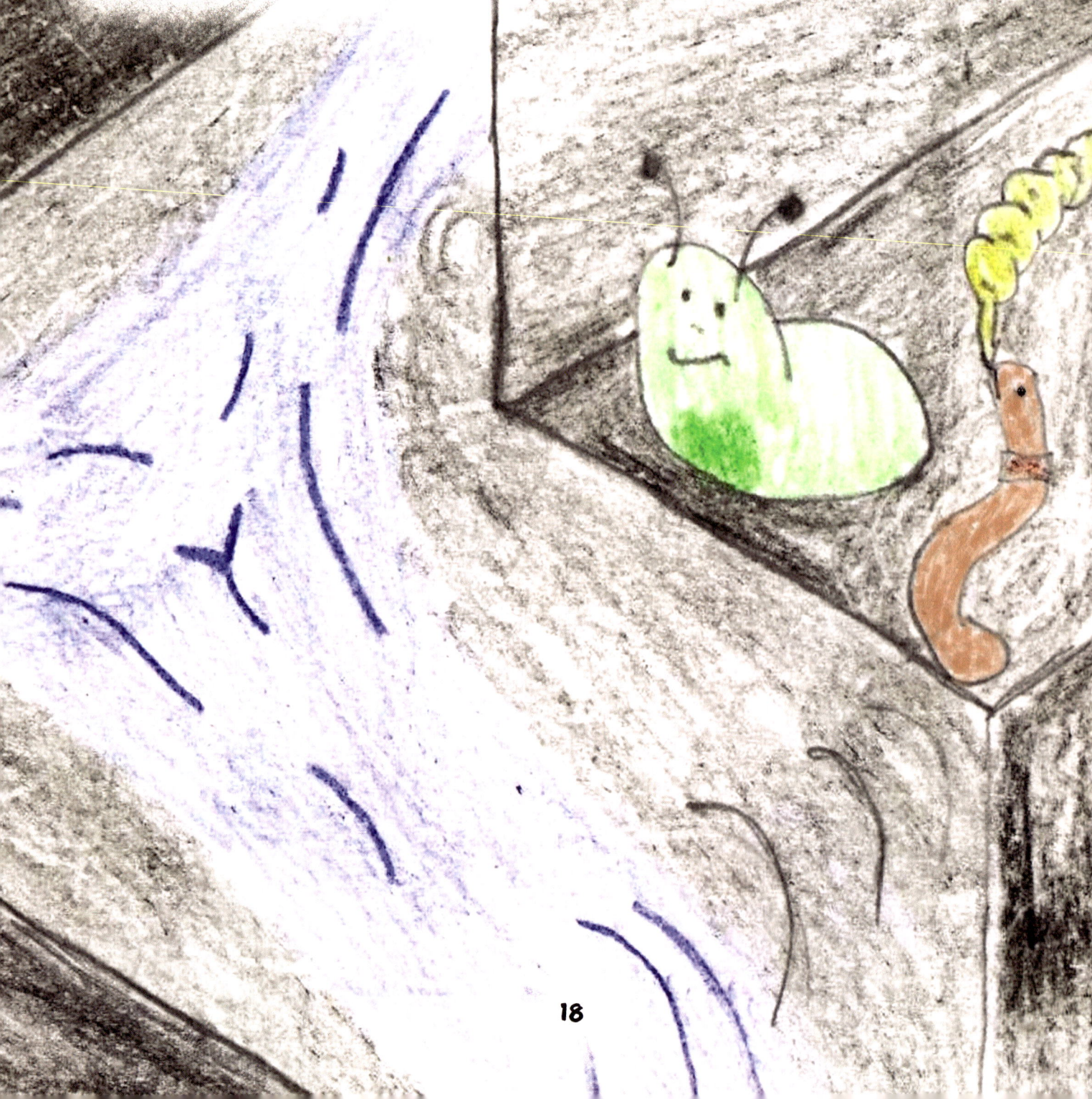

With the river's edge dying down, the three were able to escape the black hole.

Once they had escaped, they saw that they had a steep climb up the rock-like surface.

"How do we get up there?" Little Slytherly asked Mr. Slug.

"Well, one of us is going to have to hold onto Jasmine. Because I am too heavy for you to carry, so wrap yourself around me and then you can carry Jasmine."

Making sure to wrap himself snuggly onto Mr. Slug, little Slytherly held firmly onto Jasmine as they started upwards.

Clenching tightly onto Jasmine as they climbed, little Slytherly could feel himself losing grip. Struggling to hold her, he could look up and see they were almost there.

"We made it!" the exhausted Mr. Slug yelled. "Now all we have to do is cross over to the grass, where we'll be protected from the heat."

Moving quickly, they soon realized that the heat was rising faster than they had hoped.

The heat was beating on them from above and below. They struggled with each step forward. Doubt was starting to enter little Slytherly's mind. The heat was rising gradually, and they could feel their bodies begin to shrivel.

Losing strength and hopes, little Slytherly's eyes began feeling heavy with sleep. Slipping away into sleep, he saw what he thought to be Jasmine breaking free.

"Oh my gosh, you guys are cookin'!" Jasmine screamed. Swooping down onto Mr. Slug and little Slytherly, she picked them up off the scalding rock-like surface.

"It's good to see you again," whispered little Slytherly trying to smile.

Flying upward, away from the hot, rock-like surface, the two of them were very thankful that Jasmine was able to save them.

Flying towards The Great Tree, little Slytherly's hopes and dreams started to return to him.

Jasmine, barely able to carry both of them, struggled with every flap to stay airborne.

Approaching the shade of The Great Tree, all seemed well. UNTIL, A GIANT, GREAT, RED, BIRD spotted them.

"MMM... what a tasty meal." Thought the Red Bird.

"Drop us both or we will all be eaten alive!" shouted Mr. Slug.

Jasmine released them both. Falling through the air, they both could see the ground beneath them drawing closer.

THUD!!! The two of them hit the ground hard, like a pair of pinecones falling from a tree. Writhing with pain from the fall, Mr. Slug gathered himself to see if little Slytherly was okay.

"Look," little Slytherly said to Mr. Slug.

Through the thick blades of grass, the two of them could see Jasmine fleeing for her life away from the Big Red Bird.

"Hopefully Jasmine can escape and meet us at The Great Tree," said Mr. Slug to little Slytherly.

After little Slytherly and Mr. Slug were able to pick themselves up, they could see The Great Tree in the far distance.

Squinting his eyes, little Slytherly was able to see what he thought to be a door. Looking over to his right, he saw that Mr. Slug was squinting just as he was.

And so, with Jasmine protecting herself and little Slytherly wondering if his parents made it to The Great Tree, they journeyed onward.

The two soon reached The Great Tree and their suspicions were confirmed. It was a door. Drawing closer, little Slytherly began to smile again. Mr. Slug reached out, and with two knocks on the door, they could hear footsteps approaching.

The door crept open slowly, and they heard a voice speak. "Who goes there?" A voice asked.

"My friend is little Slytherly, and I am Mr. Slug."

"What is your business here?" said the voice again.

"Seeking shelter and possibly a home if you'll have me, while my friend little Slytherly lost his family in the big flood and hopes they have traveled here." Spoke Mr. Slug once again.

"Oh, Please come in then." the door opened and a male ladybug invited them inside.

Walking inside The Great Tree, little Slytherly was amazed at what he saw. The creatures living inside had built a city!

Excited, little Slytherly began searching for his parents. Moving quickly from room to room, he searched and called out to them. As each room showed no signs of his parents, he began to fear that they hadn't made it.

Sad and depressed, he walked towards a giant staircase and sat. "Little Slytherly," he heard a voice call.

Looking up the staircase, he could see his parents!

    Rushing up the staircase as quickly as he could, Little Slytherly leaped for his parents, hugging them.
    "I missed you guys so much," little Slytherly sobbed. "We missed you too. We are so proud you found your way here." said his father.
    "Slytherly," said a sweet voice. "I know that voice," thought little Slytherly. Turning around, he saw Jasmine! Happy to see her again, he hugged her as well.
    Happy to see his friends and family alive, they all began telling stories of their great adventures and how Jasmine was able to escape **THE BIG RED BIRD**.

The End.

CPSIA information can be obtained
at www.ICGtesting.com
Printed in the USA
243272LV00003B